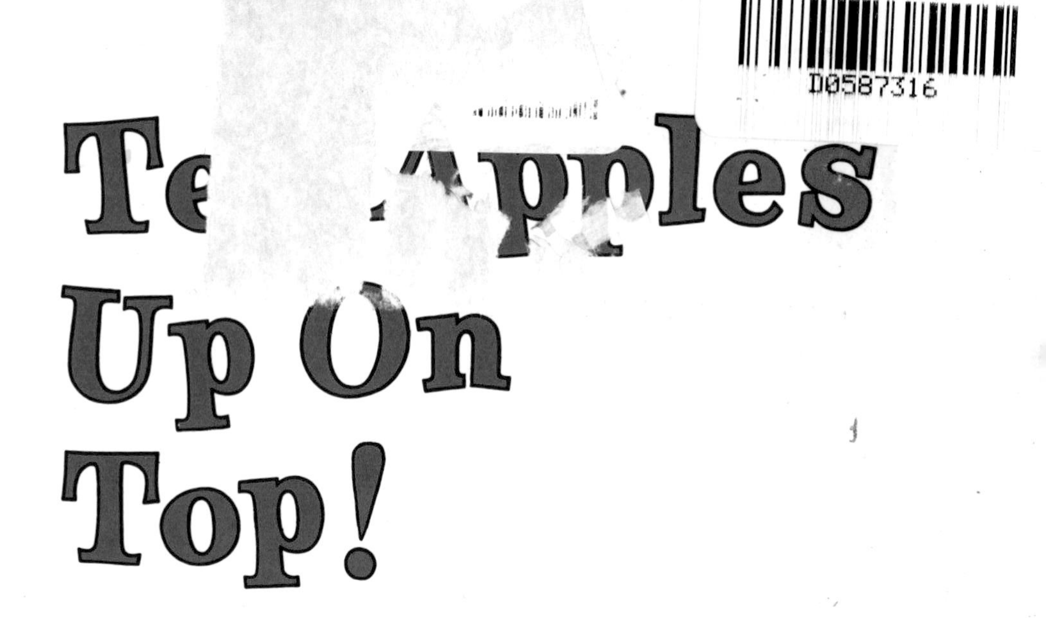

Te[illegible] [illegible]pples Up On Top!

By
Dr. Seuss
writing as
Theo. LeSieg

illustrated by Roy McKie

Collins
An imprint of HarperCollins*Publishers*

6 8 10 9 7 5

ISBN 0 00 716997 3

A Beginner Book published by arrangement with
Random House Inc., New York, USA
First published in the UK 1963
This edition published in the UK 2003 by
HarperCollins*Children's Books*,
a division of HarperCollins*Publishers* Ltd
77-85 Fulham Palace Road
London W6 8JB

Visit our website at:
www.harpercollinschildrensbooks.co.uk

Printed and bound in Hong Kong

One apple
up on top!

Two apples
up on top!

Look, you.

I can do it, too.

Look!

See!

I can do three!

Three . . .
Three . . .
I see.
I see.

You can do three
but I can do more.
You have three
but I have four.

Look! See, now.
I can hop
with four apples
up on top.

And I can hop
up on a tree
with four apples
up on me.

Look here, you two.

See here, you two.

I can get five

on top.

Can you?

I am so good
I will not stop.
Five!
Now six!
Now seven on top!

Seven apples
up on top!

I am
so good
they will not drop.

Five, six, seven!
Fun, fun, fun!
Seven, six, five,
four, three, two, one!

But, see!
We are as good as you.
Look! Now we
have seven, too.

And now, see here.

Eight! Eight on top!

Eight apples up!

Not one will drop.

Eight! Eight!
And we can skate.
Look now!
We can skate
with eight.

But I can do nine.

And hop!

And drink!

You can not do this,

I think.

We can! We can!

We can do it, too.

See here.

We are as good as you!

We all are very good
I think.
With nine, we all
can hop and drink.

Nine is very good.
But then . . .
Come on and we
will make it ten!

Look!

Ten

apples

up

on

top!

We are not

going to let them drop!

Look out!
Look out!
I see a mop.

I will make
the apples fall.
Get out. Get out. You!
One and all!

Come on! Come on!
Come down this hall.
We must not let
our apples fall!

Out of our way!
We can not stop.
We can not let
our apples drop.

This is not good.
What will we do?
They want to get
our apples, too.

They will get them
if we let them.
Come! We can not
let them get them.

Look out!

The mop!

The mop!

The mop!

You can not stop
our apple fun.
Our apples will not drop.
Not one!

Come on! Come on!
Come one! Come all!
We have to make
the apples fall.

They must not get
our apples down.
Come on! Come on!
Get out of town!

Apples!

Apples up on top!

All of this

must stop

STOP

STOP!

Now all our fun
is going to stop!
Our apples all
are going to drop.

Look!
Ten apples
on us all!

What fun!
We will not
let them fall.

1 TOKEN

The more that you read,
the more things you will know.
The more that you learn,
the more places you'll go!
– I Can Read With My Eyes Shut!

With over 30 paperbacks to collect there's a book for all ages and reading abilities, and now there's never been a better time to have fun with Dr.Seuss! Simply collect 5 tokens from the back of each Dr.Seuss book and send in for your

FREE Dr.Seuss poster

(rrp £3.99)

Send your 5 tokens and a completed voucher to:
Dr. Seuss poster offer, PO Box 142, Horsham, UK, RH13 5FJ (UK residents only)

VOUCHER

Title: Mr ☐ Mrs ☐ Miss ☐ Ms ☐

First Name:................................ Surname: ....

Address:..

Post Code:................................ E-Mail Address: ....

Date of Birth:................................ Signature of parent/guardian:................................

TICK HERE IF YOU DO NOT WISH TO RECEIVE FURTHER INFORMATION ABOUT CHILDREN'S BOOKS ☐

TERMS AND CONDITIONS: Proof of sending cannot be considered proof of receipt. Not redeemable for cash. Please allow 28 days for delivery. Photocopied tokens not accepted. Offer open to UK only.

Read them together, read them alone, read them aloud and make reading fun! With over 30 wacky stories to choose from, now it's easier than ever to find the right Dr. Seuss books for your child – just let the back cover colour guide you!

Blue back books

for sharing with your child

Dr. Seuss' ABC
The Foot Book
Hop on Pop
Mr. Brown Can Moo! Can You?
One Fish, Two Fish, Red Fish, Blue Fish
There's a Wocket in my Pocket!

Green back books

for children just beginning to read on their own

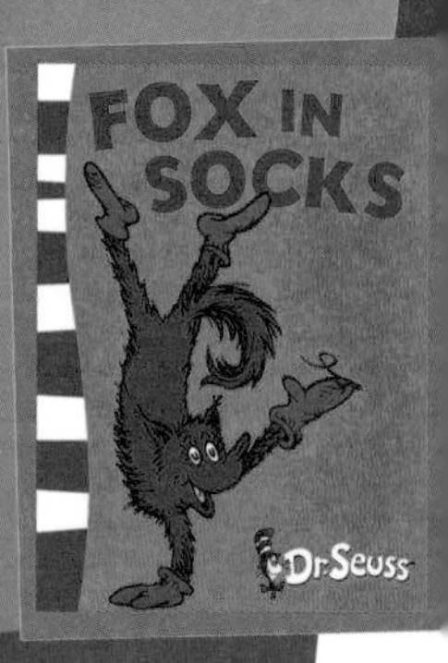

And to Think That I Saw It on Mulberry Street
The Cat in the Hat
The Cat in the Hat Comes Back
Fox in Socks
Green Eggs and Ham
I Can Read With My Eyes Shut!
I Wish That I Had Duck Feet
Marvin K. Mooney Will You Please Go Now!
Oh, Say Can You Say?
Oh, the Thinks You Can Think!
Ten Apples Up on Top
Wacky Wednesday

Yellow back books

for fluent readers to enjoy

THE SNEETCHES AND OTHER STORIES – Dr. Seuss

Daisy-Head Mayzie
Did I Ever Tell You How Lucky You Are?
Dr. Seuss' Sleep Book
Horton Hatches the Egg
Horton Hears a Who!
How the Grinch Stole Christmas!
If I Ran the Circus
If I Ran the Zoo
I Had Trouble in Getting to Solla Sollew
The Lorax
Oh, the Places You'll Go!
On Beyond Zebra
Scrambled Eggs Super!
The Sneetches and other stories
Thidwick the Big-Hearted Moose
Yertle the Turtle and other stories